MW01155812

this book belongs to:

This book is dedicated to all the little ghouls and goblins who love reading spooky books.

Thank you to Olivia, our guest illustrator!

Also, a very special dedication to Colt and Caroline. Happy birthday!
-A.M.

Meet October

Calendar Kids Books, LLC | Kathleen, GA 31047

ISBN:
(Paperback) 978-1-957161-25-9
(Hardback) 978-1-957161-26-6
Library of Congress Control Number: 2024916407

To find out more about The Calendar Kids Collection, visit www.calendarkids.com and sign up for newsletters or follow us on social media @thecalendarkids.

The Calendar Kids
Meet
OCTOBER
April Martin

This is October.

October loves the cool fall days and the pretty colors of the leaves in his yard. He loves the pumpkins they pick each year and the jack-o'-lanterns they make with them too!

October loves going on fall camping trips with his family. They hike, watch football games, get lost in the corn maze, and look for the biggest pumpkin at the pumpkin patch.

This year, they brought October's closest friends, September and November! October was so excited to pick out pumpkins with his friends! They planned to look at every pumpkin in the patch. They were going to hunt for the biggest pumpkin of all.

It didn't take them long to find the best pumpkin in the patch.
"Ouch!" October shouts. "That's not a pumpkin! That's me!"

September, October, and November giggle the whole way back to the campsite. The friends were happy they found the best pumpkins in the patch, but now their fall camping trip was coming to an end. On Monday they would start another week at school.

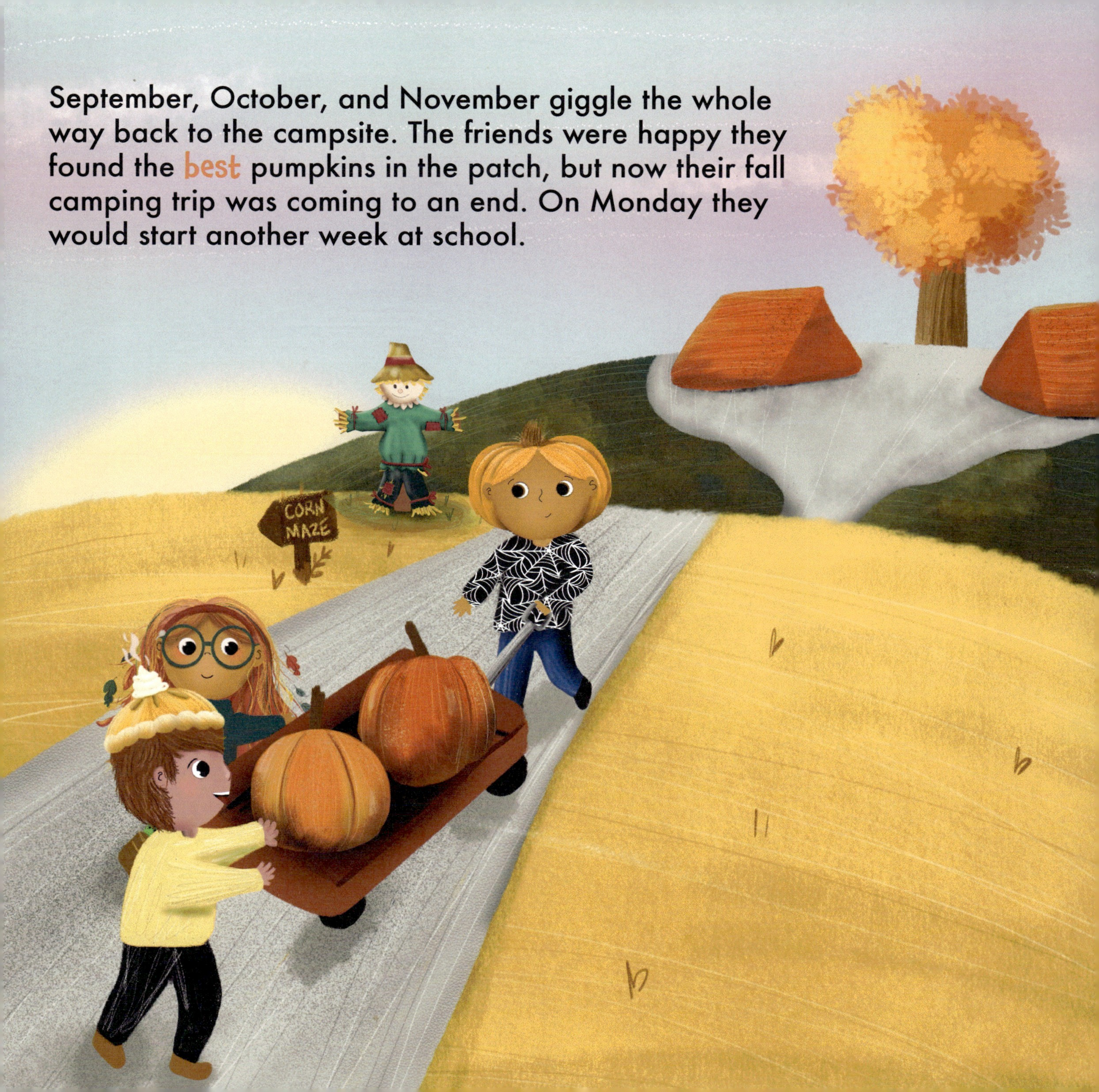

"Do you think you can make it past the spooky house on the way to school?" November asks. "I bet it has even more scary decorations up now!"

“Oh no,” October sighs. “I bet you’re right. I guess I will just try to be brave.”

What October doesn't like are the really spooky things all around town. Every day he sees the extra spooky house on his walk home from school and runs as fast as he can to hide from it.

It even ruins his afternoons because he is so scared. He wants to play with his friends, but first he has to come out from under the covers.

Then, he has to grab a scarf to hide from the spooky house.

He tries to be brave. It takes him a really long time to be ready to play. Plus, he looks **really** silly.

The next morning, October's sister had a surprise for him before he left for school. She made his favorite fall food, pumpkin muffins, for breakfast.

When October woke up, he got dressed for the cool fall morning. He ate his pumpkin muffins, said bye to Boo, his pet spider, and walked QUICKLY to school.

"Oh no," he thought. "There it is! I can do this. I can do this! I WILL be brave!"

He took one peek at the spooky house and ran all the way home. “NOPE! Not today! November was right! It’s even spookier now!”

By the time October made it home, he was out of breath.
He couldn't speak.

He couldn't bear the thought of going outside again. It didn't help that it was foggy outside, and the house was the spookiest it had ever been!

Thankfully, his older sister was still home and asked him if he was ok. He told her about the spooky house down the road.

"Oh October, those silly decorations aren't real. Come on. I'll walk with you to school! Let's go!"

October held on tight to the door. He didn't want to go. He couldn't imagine walking past the spooky house again. He would rather be at the pumpkin patch getting mistaken for a pumpkin again more than this!

October's sister giggled. "Come on scaredy cat, let's go. You're going to be late for school!" On the way out the door he grabbed his pet spider, Boo, to join him on the walk too!

The fog was going away as they walked to school, and October wasn't as scared as he thought he would be.

"I like feeling brave," October thought. It helped being around his sister and a friend!

In science class that day, his teacher Ms. Seasons taught the class all about bats and owls.

And because he brought Boo to school with him, they had a show-and-tell to learn about spiders too!

He even learned why the leaves were starting to fall off the trees at the playground and what kind of critters can be found in a leaf pile. It was a really fun day of learning.

All of a sudden, October heard a bunch of screaming!

"Ahhh! Spiiiiiderrrrrr!"

"Oh no, Boo! Boo! Where are you?" October shouted.

The class made a mess running from the spider. October looked all over for his pet. He couldn't see him anywhere! Boo was too small.

At the end of the day, October still could not find Boo. He was so sad.

September and November told him it would be ok.
“You will find him soon. Don’t worry friend!”

"Did you know a spider's eyes twinkle at night?" October asked. "I read about it in a book today. Wait–that gives me an idea!"

On the way home, September, October, and November made a plan to find Boo. The sun would be setting soon. They would grab flashlights and start looking for him at night.

October ran to his home so fast,

past the spooky house
without even noticing,

and grabbed his flashlight.

First, they passed a bunch of kids in costumes. October thought they looked more silly than scary. “Have you seen a black spider anywhere?” he asked.

The kids shook their heads no, so off he went to look some more.

BoO!

Ahh!

BoO!

Ahhhhh!

"Why did you have to name him Boo?" November asked. "Now I'm sc-sc-scared".

October giggled, but he knew it was time to go to the spooky house again—this time at night! October was afraid of the dark. This was too scary, but losing his pet was even scarier!

He spotted some eyes up in the tree.

"Ahhhhhhh! What's that?"

He shined his light and spotted an owl.

"Hoo... hoo," she said.
"Oh, hi, Mrs. Owl. Just me,"
October replied.

Next, he heard some flapping in the wind.

"Ahhhhhhh! What was that?"

He shined his light and saw a bat.

"Oh, hi, Mr. Bat... you're not very scary to me anymore. I know all about owls and bats, and now I'm brave!"

Finally, October was at the spooky house. It looked *extra* creepy. It was *covered* with cobwebs. Plus, he lost track of his friends in the dark and he was all alone. October decided it was time to be as brave as he could be.

GULP!

So he flashed his light at the house.

One by one, he spotted little bits of glitter... he peeked in for a closer look and spotted a set of spider eyes, but it wasn't Boo.

He shined his light high and found another set of glittery eyes.
“Boo! There you are! What are you doing here in this big web?” he asked.

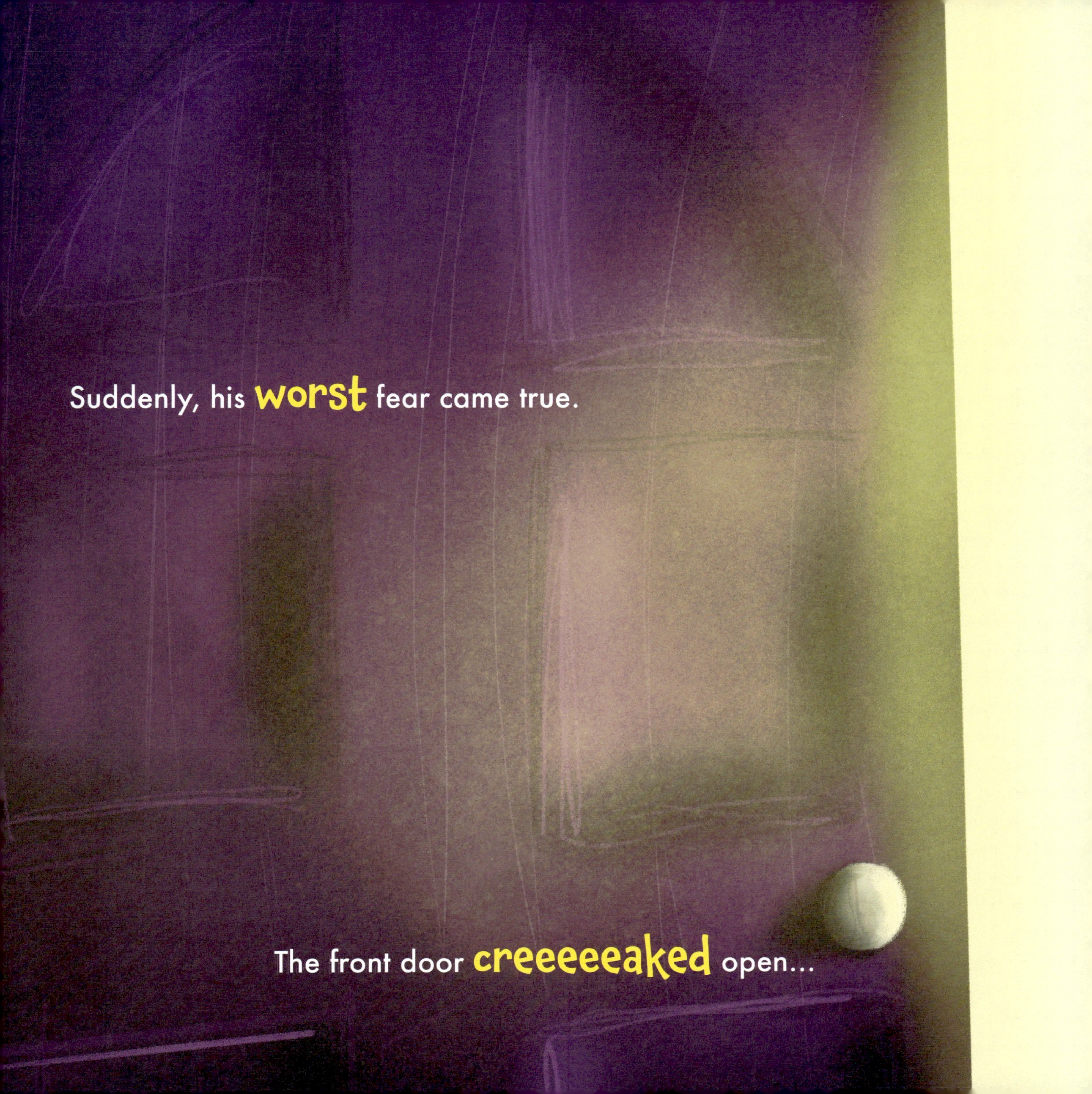

Suddenly, his **worst** fear came true.

The front door **creeeeeaked** open...

Slowly, Mr. Cal Ender, the principal from school, peeked his head out. "Hi, October! I found Boo in the halls after school and thought I would keep him safe in our web decoration! He seems to like it here!"

October was feeling brave...
until he was spooked once again!

My October Notebook

Special October birthdays or events in my family:

The best part about the month of October is...

October is the tenth month of the year.
October has 31 days.
The month after October is November.
The first Wednesday in October is National Walk to School Day.
October is National Principals Month.
If you are born in October, your birthstone is the opal or tourmaline.
Many people enjoy wearing costumes on October 31st for Halloween.
October is a fall month.

Discussion Questions

1. October goes on a fall camping trip with his family. Have you ever been camping? What do you do at your campsite?

2. Do you pick your own pumpkins from a pumpkin patch? If not, do you pick them out at the store?

3. October thought the fog made the spooky house even scarier. What is fog?

4. Are you afraid of the dark? What is spooky to you? What can you do to be brave like October?

5. Did you know you can spot spider eyes with a flashlight? What other animals can you see better at night with a light?

6. Why do you think October was so scared at the end of the story?

So Easy, It's Spooky Pumpkin Muffins

You will need:

1 box of yellow or white cake mix
1 15 oz can of pumpkin puree
1 handful of chocolate chips
2 teaspoons of pumpkin pie spice
brown or white sugar for toppings
muffin liners

1. Preheat the oven to 350°F. Add liners to a muffin tin.
2. Have a grown up open the can of pumpkin puree.
3. Open the box of cake mix and dump it into a large mixing bowl.
4. Add the pumpkin puree and pumpkin pie spice to the cake mix. Mix by hand with a spoon.
5. Spoon the mixture into the muffin liners. We like to fill them almost to the top.
6. Top each muffin with a sprinkle of brown or white sugar.
7. Add one chocolate chip to the top of each muffin. This will be your pumpkin "stem."
8. Bake for 20 minutes. Check to make sure the muffin is cooked through by inserting a toothpick through the center of a muffin. The toothpick should come out clean.

Author April Martin loves the fall! She loves all things spooky too! She even had a pet tarantula in her classroom. Yikes! She enjoys cool fall nights and camping with her family. Every fall, her family looks for the best pumpkin at the pumpkin patch.

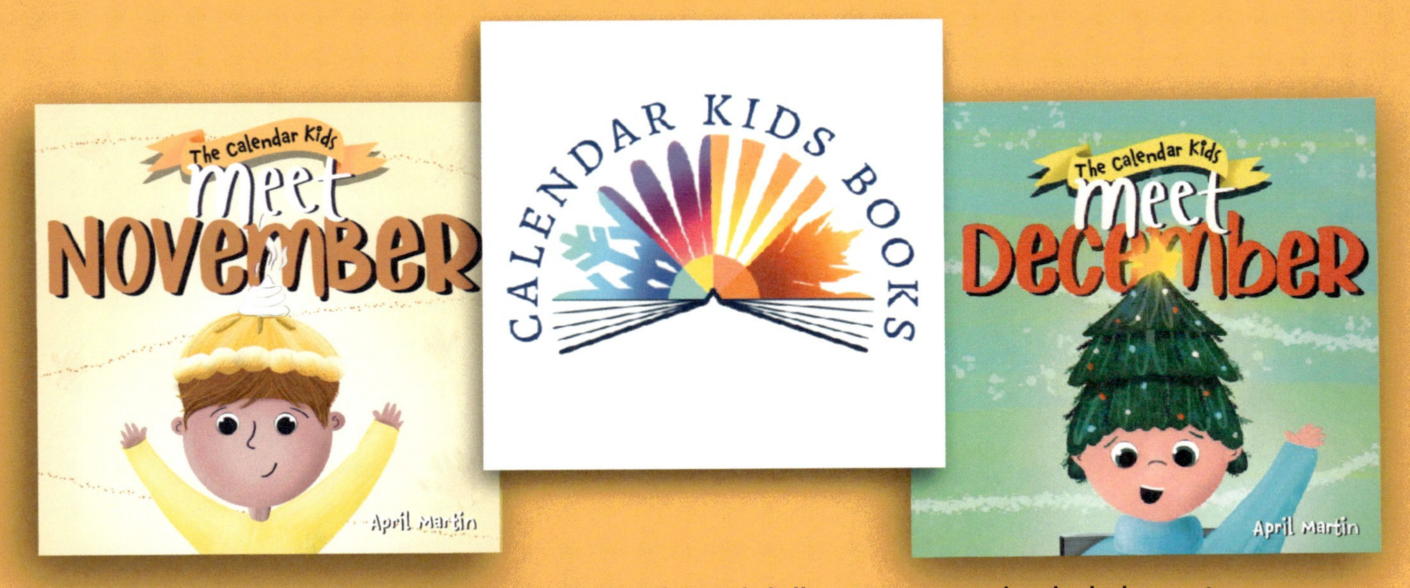

To learn more about Calendar Kids® books and dolls, visit www.calendarkids.com!